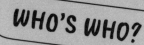

WHO'S WHO?

ANDY! Schoolkid and secret superhero

Awesome rating: THE AWESOMEST

MONA! Andy's best friend and tech genius

Awesome rating: ELEVEN OUT OF TEN

OSCAR! Andy's annoying little brother

Awesome rating: NOT VERY

MEAN MIKE! A school bully

Awesome rating: THE EXACT OPPOSITE OF AWESOME

THE PENCIL OF DESTINY!

A radioactive pencil that can bring doodles to life!

Awesome rating: OFF THE SCALE

CONTENTS

Chapter 1   **The Legend of Super Dweeb**

- -

HEY THERE, READER! Have we met before? You look kind

of familiar. (Just joking, I 100% can't see you through the book.

Don't look so nervous!)

My name's **ANDY**. I'm nearly eleven,

and I'm pretty awesome at drawing.

However, I'm not super-great at talking

to strangers, and sometimes I get a little

OBSESSIVE about stuff.

According to some people, this makes

me a **DWEEB**. But that's where

they're wrong. I'm not a dweeb—

I'm a **SUPER DWEEB!**

My *SECRET SUPERHERO ORIGIN* began with

a field trip to a toxic waste dump. (Yes,

my teacher makes some weird choices.)

A squirrel stole my pencil and they both

fell into a weird substance called

BLOOTONIUM!

The Blootonium gave my pencil POWERS and it brings my drawings to LIFE!

My best friend Mona talked me into becoming a SUPERHERO.

A shady agency called A.C.R.O.N.Y.M. started spying on me. A scientist working there stole some of my eraser shavings and turned himself into a VILLAIN:

DR. ERASER-BUTT!

Mona and I defeated him with help from a non-evil super spy called AGENT STORM. She's great! And a bit terrifying!

Agent Storm was so impressed by Mona that she offered her a super-spy internship. And Mona accepted it, so that she can keep an eye on A.C.R.O.N.Y.M.

As I was saying, I can get a <u>TINY BIT</u> obsessive. Mona calls it my "sticky brain." The latest thing that I'm into is Snackamon cards. They're super-collectable Japanese trading cards and **I NEED EVERY SINGLE ONE OF THEM!!!**

Ahem. As I was saying, I get a little obsessive. But I don't let it affect my superhero work.

Hey, bank robber! You're as bad as the common Snackamon card, Mouse Melon!

Welcome to the bank!

Ugh, Mouse Melon! I've got SEVEN and no one will trade with me.

No way! I've got an extra Eggplant. Got any other cards to swap?

Do you need a Chowder Chaff?

Eh, excuse me — you're supposed to be stopping the bank robber!

Bank teller! ↓

Okay, so Snackamon might have taken over my life temporarily but so what? Everyone at school is into them. I mean, just look how cool they are! We're not really meant to have them in class ...

CORNDOG	EGGIPLANT	POTATOAD	NOODLECROC

He'll batter you good!	What will he hatch into?	Good stats and good starch!	UDON want to tangle with him!

My card collection is nearly 150 strong and I hide them in my history book!

Uh...!

← Random classmate!

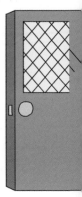

What Mr. Squibb doesn't know won't hurt him. When it comes to Snackamon cards, I'm very smart!

—Andy ...

7

"Well, Andy, if you're so smart how about sharing with the class what an oxbow lake is?" said Mr. Squibb.

"Uh, a lake full of cows with bows and arrows?" I chanced.

"Wow, that's exactly right!" Mr. Squibb exclaimed.

"Oh, really? PHEW!" I said.

"No, not really!!" Mr. Squibb EXPLODED. "Not even remotely really! I've had it up to here with those Snackamon cards. From right this minute, they are BANNED!"

NOOOOOOOOOOOOOOOOOOOO!!

Dreams shattered!

Most terrible thing!

World ended!

Mildly inconvenienced!

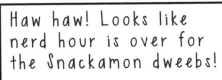

Haw haw! Looks like nerd hour is over for the Snackamon dweebs!

Class bully ← Mean Mike!

Yeah, well ... shut up!

Catastrophic comeback fail!

You are _so_ lame.

C'mon, brain!

Yeah? At least I didn't think the capital of England was E!

That was an honest mistake!

Chapter 2 **Future Shock!**

Meanwhile, in the year 2049 …

… things are pretty great.

Videogames are a mandatory part of schoolwork.

There are robots and flying cars.

Cabbage tastes slightly better.

But the future is TERRIBLE for bad guys like me! We're all in super-jail thanks to a meddlesome superhero called SUPER DWEEB!

I'm older and wiser and I can draw hands really well.

Future facial hair!

Some supervillains have had enough.

FUTURE JAIL
(No escaping please!)

Grr, I HATE Super Dweeb!

Me too!

Doc Clock

Combat Wombat

Robo-Bonobo

He's ruined everything! Nowadays, honest, hard-working bad guys like us just can't get a break.

Tell me about it! The market for marsupial mercenaries just isn't there any more.

OOK BEE POOK EEE!

A very eloquent point, Robo-Bonobo.

I couldn't agree more.

Pick!

11

If only there was some way out of this mess! Wait, your name is Doc Clock! Aren't you some kind of time-travel guy?

Yeah, but I don't have my super stuff here. This clock just tells the time!

Do you not have wrists?!

Eeek! Oook! Beep!

No, I don't think that's anatomically possible.

Someone's coming!

Clip clop clip clop

Well, Doc Clock, it looks like your henchmen sent you a present!

Happy birthday!

But it's not your— oof!

Now the guard has gone, my fellow felons, I can show you the true source of my power ...

Plunge!

With this, we can travel to the past and stop this stupid future from happening!

PARP! BZEW!

But it's still not your birthday!

Yah!!

Yank!

13

15

In Andy's room ...

Beep!
Boop!

So how's the superheroing going?

Pretty good! I got a rare Snackamon card from a bad guy.

Andy! That's not very superheroic!

It's fine. What did you want to tell me about A.C.R.O.N.Y.M.?

Well, I'm sure they're up to something, but I only have two days left of my internship and they've changed all the access passwords!

Well, at least you still have that coffee drone you stole!

BORROWED!!

"Here's what we know so far," said Mona. "A.C.R.O.N.Y.M. have sent agents to FALLOUT ISLAND—that's where you got your powers. And they've been transporting something in crates."

"So … what do you think is in the crates?" I asked.

"Mutant creatures, maybe? Or BLOOTONIUM?"

"If we knew where they were going, we could sneak in. Can you try to hack the passwords one more time?"

"MONA!" Mom called up the stairs, "Your dad is here to pick you up!"

"Right," said Mona, "I'll give it one more try at A.C.R.O.N.Y.M. to see if I can find anything!"

Team Dweeb

High Five!

The next day, at the mysterious top-secret headquarters of A.C.R.O.N.Y.M. ...

Super secret!

Don't look!

You don't have clearance!

So much for finding out anything ...

I've had to replace the missing coffee drone as coffee maker.

Hey, coffee drone! Hit me up with a caramel latte.

Ugh, this guy again!

Sure thing, sir...!

Mumble!

Don't worry, coffee drone. If you work hard for years you'll get to where I am!

Smug!

18

19

Thanks for the coffee. But I need you for something else.

Does it have to do with Fallout Island?

Ha, you're a bright one! Yes, and believe me, this isn't something I'm okay with!

Well, can't you do anything about it? I thought you were the head honcho!

Unfortunately not! I can't say too much, but ...

A.C.R.O.N.Y.M. were ordered to take over Fallout Island by THE DIRECTOR!

Who's the Director?

Come on, we'll talk on the way.

Wait, is this a FLYING submarine?!

21

Chapter 3 The End of Super Dweeb

Snackamon?
Snackamon!
Snackamon ...

... and if
you all turn
to page 157
in your ...

Now that school was a Snackamon-free zone, I was completely drained of any sense of purpose. What did I even DO before trading cards came into my life?! Then, suddenly, I saw something through the classroom window ...

BANK

Is that ... an awesome portal?

I had to act fast! This was a job for Super Dweeb!

"Can't you wait?" Mr. Squibb sighed.

"But, Taco Tuesday!" I said, squirming in my seat.

Mr. Squibb grimaced. "T.M.I., ANDY! Go on, then."

I raced to my locker to get my suit and pencil. I drew a dupe and loaded him with pencils to send him back to class with.

At the bank ...

Oh good, we're on a bank!

We need some change— our future cash won't work here!

You idiot, we're not robbing the bank! It's a trap! We're here to stop Super Dweeb before he can make our future a misery.

Oh, right!

And here he comes!

Woah, you guys are all dressed weird! Where are you from?!

He's so young!

Thanks for asking! We're criminals from the future.

Shut up, Wombat!

25

Doc Clock, help! His doodles are crude but effective!

Don't worry, I know past Super Dweeb's one weakness thanks to the history books ...

... SNACKAMON CARDS!

Uh-oh!

No way! Rare titanium foil cards ... from the future!

That's right—these are completely unique. Best cards EVER.

Ooooh!

Best of all, they're scratch-and-sniff.

Eep!

27

29

I trudged back to school, not even caring if my dupe had disappeared, My pencil was gone. Who am I if I don't have my pencil?!

Wistful walk!

Luckily, it was time for lunch when I made it back to school.

"Hey," said Mean Mike, "I thought Dweebo was still inside! How did he get out here so quickly?"

HEY DWEEB-FACE! Where are your itty-bitty Snackamon cards? Heh!

I didn't care what Mean Mike was talking about.

All I could think was that I was...

SUPER DWEEB NO MORE!

Meanwhile...

This is pretty neat!

It comes in handy. One of the perks of being a secret agent!

So what's the deal? Why let me in on what's going on at Fallout Island?

Ever since A.C.R.O.N.Y.M. first heard about Super Dweeb's atomic pencil, we've been trying to make atomic WEAPONS. You showed me how wrong that is.

And I take it this is all because of the Director? Who are they?

It's so top level, even I don't know! And I don't like that one bit.

Hmpf, they've been busy!

Welcome, Agent Storm.

EVIL BUTT GUY!

Did I say that out loud?

The last time I saw you, you were trying to erase the world with your butt.

Yeah well, the Director of A.C.R.O.N.Y.M. gave me another chance!

Hmmmm!

Well, Agent Storm and guest! Let me show you around our new facility! And just to be clear ...

... I am no longer evil in any way!

Eyeball twitch!

Sure.

We are using this island's reserves of Blootonium to attempt to replicate Super Dweeb's pencil!

And we are investigating the effects of Blootonium on other random objects, too. Look!

Grr!

Here is where we saturate high levels of Blootonium into everyday objects!

Behold!

And what have you concluded from all of this?

The results have been less than satisfactory. Nothing has come close to Super Dweeb's pencil!

So far we've made ...

... a hat with no shadow!

A teddy bear that knows what you had for lunch!

Fishsticks.

A glowing trumpet!

Well, this seems less terrifying than I had expected.

Hmm!

35

I just cannot figure out what the missing element is that makes the original pencil so powerful! My only theory is that Super Dweeb himself is the missing piece to activating these objects!

The key to power!

That seems like quite a leap.

I don't like where this is going!

If we can capture Super Dweeb, hook him up to our machines and harvest his molecules ...

WHAT?!

Don't even get me started on the ethics of that!

Super Dweeb is a good person! You don't get to experiment on him! And A.C.R.O.N.Y.M. shouldn't be doing experiments if you have no idea what will even happen!

That evening, Mona and I were playing board games at her house.

It was **BAD NEWS** all round.

"This is terrible!" said Mona. "Your pencil is broken and A.C.R.O.N.Y.M. are on the way to using <u>YOU</u> to make new weapons!"

"This is awful!" I wailed. "I don't know who I am any more, without my pencil!"

"I'M HAVING AN <u>IDENTITY CRISIS!</u>"

"Those STUPID bad guys from the future and their STUPID, weird glowing trumpet." I said.

"Wait," said Mona, "Did you say they had a GLOWING TRUMPET?"

"Yeah, that stupid egg guy used it and then it broke!"

I KNEW IT!

"Dr. Sidebottom is back working at A.C.R.O.N.Y.M.!" said Mona, "At some point he's gonna turn <u>EVIL</u> again and use that trumpet to travel back in time to defeat you!"

"Mona, you're so smart to figure this all out!"

"Well, it wasn't too hard! Based on your description, Doctor Eraser-Butt and Doc Clock look exactly the same!"

OBVIOUS!

"We need a plan to get that trumpet! It seems as if you'll be able to activate it somehow. Like, some kind of DWEEB PARTICLES you have inside you makes these objects work!" said Mona.

Ooh, dweeb particles!

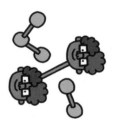

"Gah, if only I hadn't quit the internship, we could have easily visited the island! New plan time."

MONA'S TIME TRUMPET PLAN!

Step 1! Okay! We get Captain Poopdeck to take us back to Fallout Island.

But first... A NEW PLAN WARNING!

Step 2! We use my borrowed coffee drone to grab the trumpet!

You mean "STOLEN!"   No, "BORROWED!"

Step 3! Then, we travel back in time to right before your pencil got broken and use the trumpet to send the bad guys back to the future!

"Aaaaah! I get it now!"

"We just have to make sure we don't run into your past self and cause a paradox that destroys the Universe!" said Mona.

"Is that a thing that can happen?!" I squeaked.

"Yes, but don't overthink it. Here's what we need you to do ..."

Chapter 5 *The Time Trumpet*

And so...

Thanks for helping us, Captain! You're always conveniently available to take us where we need to go!

Yar, no problem! I'm happy to help you young land-lubbers!

But first...
A WARNING!

Uh, I think we know what to expect from these voyages now, Captain!

No, a warning about the deck! I just had it waxed!

Yah!

Slip!

Soon...

Okay, let's get that trumpet!

Engage stealth mode!

FUNCTION NOT FOUND!

Why would a coffee drone have a stealth mode, Andy?

Bot, I'll have a caramel latte! Hey! HEY!

Ignore him!

Okay... steady... steady...

Got it! Quick, run!

43

Okay, so I guess you need to activate it!

Uh, how?

ACTIVATE! WORK! Uh ... please?

Maybe I should just mash the buttons?

Andy, no!

Mash! Bash!

We need to make sure we arrive at the right point in time! If we don't do it right, we could end up somewhere dangerous!

Beep! Toot!

Parp.

BZZZZZT!

AAAAAAAHHHHHHH!

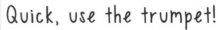

We need some time to accurately assess of our space-time coordinates. And rest!

CHING!

Hurk!

Uh, I think I can take a pretty good guess as to where in time we are.

Are you not entertained?!

No, I am not entertained, thank you very much!

PARP!

Come on!

Yah!

I can't look! Where are we now?

It's not too bad! I think we're in the 1980s?

Oh, my parents told me about the 80s! There was no wifi back then!

NOOOOOOOO!

And...

Okay, we finally have the right coordinates in time! Let's go!

Parp!!

Yes! We're here! There's past me fighting them on the roof of the bank!

"Now we need to stop them before they throw my pencil away!" I said.

"No! We can't, we have to wait until it gets thrown. We can't risk you meeting your past self. It could cause a major rift in space and TEAR THE UNIVERSE APART!" said Mona.

Oh yeah, I forgot I could destroy the Universe.

Yeah, that!

"This is a lot of pressure for a 10-year-old kid!" I mused.

Quick, hide behind that dumpster. We can't risk Past Andy seeing us with the pencil.

Okay, we need to draw a broken pencil for Past Andy to find. We'll keep the REAL pencil!

Hee hee!

Quick! Here you ... ah ... he ... Super Dweeb comes!

Don't worry, Past Andy! I know it all feels bad now but things will get better!

Grr! Well, we'll break it again.

I'll calibrate the trumpet to the future, you distract them.

Gladly!

Okay, future fools!

PEN CIL

GO!

Battle peas!

Explosively flatulent bean!

Chicken with a supersonic cluck!

Perturbed two-headed dog!

57

Maybe it became a paradox of itself and got swallowed up in its own temporal vortex?

?!?!

Oh, I'm not even going to pretend that I know what I'm talking about!

Actually the trumpet got sent one minute into the future, somehow!

So, my theory was correct!

Fzzzt!

Ominous music!

Evil eye twitch!

Bzzzt!

What will happen now that Dr. Sidebottom has the time trumpet? Oh wait, we already know! Gah, time-travel plots!

"So, I'm guessing we prevented any
paradoxes and preserved the timeline,"
I said to Mona as we walked home.

"I think so," said Mona.
"I guess the trumpet ended
up in the right place because
nothing drastic has happened."

"So is Past Andy going to travel
to the island with Past Mona and
steal the trumpet, then fight
those bad guys all over again?"
I asked.

"You know what,"
Mona said, "it's best
not to think about
it too hard!"

"Did I miss anything exciting while I was at science camp?" shouted Oscar.

"Not really," I said. "At PRESENT, we're just hanging out. The FUTURE might be more exciting but at the moment we're PAST caring!"

"I don't believe it," whined Oscar. "I missed some amazing Super Dweeb adventure!"

"Here," I said and handed Oscar my entire Snackamon card collection. "There are even a few super-rare future cards in there!"